Aristotle

DICK KING-SMITH

illustrated by
Bob Graham

**WALKER
BOOKS**

Chapter One

When Aristotle was a kitten, he did not know that cats have nine lives. His mother knew, of course. But I'm not going to tell him, she thought. Already he's a tearaway, much bolder than his brothers and sisters, and if he knows that he's got nine lives to play with, he'll take all sorts of risks.

So she didn't say anything to

Aristotle except "Goodbye" when he left home and went to live with an old lady.

A strange looking old lady she was, with a beaky nose and a chin that jutted out, and she wore black clothes and a tall black hat on top of her stringy grey hair.

Her name was Bella Donna, and it was she who decided to call her new kitten Aristotle.

Aristotle

For Zona ~ D. K-S.
To Caitlin and her coven ~ B. G.

First published 2003 by Walker Books Ltd
87 Vauxhall Walk, London SE11 5HJ

This edition published 2014

2 4 6 8 10 9 7 5 3 1

Text © 2003 Foxbusters Ltd
Illustrations © 2003, 2013 Blackbird Design Pty Ltd

This book has been typeset in Bembo Regular

Printed and bound in Great Britain by Clays Ltd, St Ives plc

British Library Cataloguing in Publication Data:
a catalogue record for this book is available from the British Library

ISBN 978-1-4063-5436-2

www.walker.co.uk

"Really," she said,
"I ought to have a black
cat, but it'll be a nice
change to have a white one."

But the very first day that
Aristotle went to live in Bella
Donna's funny old cottage, he
decided he would explore it from
top to bottom. Or rather from
bottom to top, because when he'd
looked all round the downstairs

rooms and then the upstairs rooms, he thought he'd like to get up on the roof.

It was a thatched roof, so, once Aristotle climbed up the creeper that grew on the walls of the cottage, he could easily walk up the thatch to the single chimney. Then, because he was curious, as all cats are, he scrambled up the chimney-stack and looked down

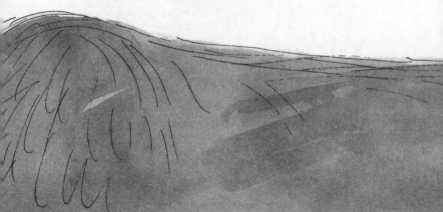

the chimney-pot and wondered
what the hole in it was for.

At that very moment a big
puff of smoke came up, right in
Aristotle's face, which made him
cough and sneeze and lose his
balance, and down the chimney
he fell.

Bella Donna had just lit her
kitchen fire when down into the
fireplace came a great load of soot,
which put out the flames,

and after the soot, a kitten that had

been white but was now black

as a witch's hat.

"Well, my boy," said Bella Donna, "that's the first of your nine lives gone. Good job the chimney was so dirty or you'd have burned to death. You'd better be a bit more careful, Aristotle, if you want to grow to be a cat. Only eight to go."

Chapter Two

There was a fair old bit of tidying up to do after that. Using a large broomstick that stood in a corner of her kitchen, Bella Donna swept up all the mess that the fall of soot had made. Then she laid the fire again and lit it. Then she heated some water on it, which, when warm enough, she poured into a big tin basin. Then she picked up

Aristotle and put him in the basin and rinsed him and soaped him and rinsed him again.

Aristotle had mixed feelings about all this. On the one hand, like all cats, he hated being dirty and it was lovely to be a white kitten again. On the other, he hated water. But once Bella Donna had rubbed him dry and set before him a dish of meat, he decided that his new owner meant him more good than harm.

Aristotle did not know what

the meat was (it was in fact a mixture of frogs' legs, snails and fried woodlice), but he thought it was delicious. He cleared the dish, lay down in front of the fire and fell fast asleep.

When he woke up again it was to find himself alone. The old lady had gone, shutting the kitchen door behind her, and so, he noticed, had her broomstick.

Where she had gone he did not know, but what with the big meal he had eaten and the heat of the

fire, Aristotle began to feel very
thirsty. He set off to explore the
kitchen for something to drink.

On a table, his eyes told him,
stood a large heavy earthenware
jug. He jumped up and peered into
it. It was, his nose told him, full of
milk of some sort, though from

which animal he did not know
(it was in fact a mixture of cow's
milk, goat's milk and ewe's milk,
with a dash of pigeon's milk added).

He put a paw down into the
jug and stirred the liquid around,
which, his ears told him, made an
appetizing sloshy sound. He pulled

out the paw and licked it and his
tongue told him that it tasted
delightful.

Eagerly Aristotle put both paws
on the rim of the jug and shoved
his head down inside it and began

greedily to drink. As the level of
the milk dropped, so he pushed
more of himself into the heavy
jug, until at last it tipped over on
top of him.

When, just after midnight,
Bella Donna came back, she opened
the kitchen door, propped her
broomstick in the corner and then
heard a most melancholy mewing.

By the dying light of the fire,
she could see that her great
earthenware milk jug was standing
upside down in the middle of the

kitchen table, that there was milk all over both table and floor, and that the noise was coming from inside the upturned jug.

Lighting a candle, she lifted the jug to reveal beneath it a whiter than white, wetter than wet, woebegone kitten.

Once more she warmed water to wash Aristotle. Once more she rubbed him dry. Once more she addressed him.

"Well, my boy," said Bella Donna, "that's the second of your

lives gone. Good job the jug tipped
over or you'd have stuck in it, head
down, and drowned. You'd better
be a bit more careful, Aristotle, or
you'll never make old bones. Only
seven lives to go."

Dry and warm now, the
white kitten looked up at
the black-clothed old woman
and felt strangely comforted by
the sound of her voice.

Chapter Three

Before she went to bed, Bella put Aristotle out in the garden.

"I expect you drank a lot of that milk," she said to him, "and there's been enough mess in the kitchen without you adding to it." What a rascal he is, she said to herself. He only came here yesterday but already he's used up two lives. At this rate, he'll never grow into a proper witch's cat.

But in fact Aristotle managed to keep out of trouble for quite a while. A whole week went by and the white kitten behaved sensibly. He ate his meat and drank his milk and didn't scratch at the curtains or the chair covers and didn't make any messes in the cottage.

Indeed, by the end of that week Bella Donna had trained him to use a dirt tray.

"You didn't make a very good start, Aristotle," she said to him, "but now you're doing fine. Just keep on keeping out of mischief." And she crossed her long knobbly fingers.

If Aristotle had gone to an ordinary home things might have been different, but Bella's old cottage was in many ways a risky sort of place for an adventurous kitten.

It stood in the middle of a little wood in which were many tall trees, and through which flowed a swift steep-banked stream. On one side of the wood there was a twisty road, and on the other a lofty embankment along the top of which ran a railway line. There was also a farm nearby, on which lived a large dog.

Aristotle's next adventure took place up a tall tree. Climbing was something he found he rather liked, and he often now scrambled up the creeper on the cottage walls and up the thatched roof to sit upon the ridge-pole at the top (though he kept away from the chimney-pot). He enjoyed this lofty perch but the cottage was quite a low building and the trees around it were, he could see, much higher.

So one fine morning, Aristotle chose a tall tree and leapt up its trunk onto the lowest branch, and then onto a higher one, and so on, up and up, feeling such a clever cat.

But the further up he went, the thinner and more springy the branches became, till at last he found himself right at the top, clinging to a thin bough that danced in the breeze,

and he suddenly felt ever such
a scared kitten. The ground, he
could see, was an awful long way
down, and the wind seemed to be
getting stronger and the bough
bouncier. He lost his nerve, and
his grip, gave a loud yowl of fright
and fell.

By good fortune, Bella Donna
was looking out of her open
kitchen window and heard her
kitten's cries and saw him fall,
paws spread wide, tail whirling
madly round and round, down,

down, down, bumping off the
branches as he went.

Let's hope
he lands in the
stream, she thought,
and she grabbed
her broomstick
and hurried out.

Luck was on Aristotle's side,
for he did indeed land, with a
great splash, in water that was very
cold and running very fast. He
swallowed a lot of it as he struggled
and spluttered and tried in vain to
scramble up the stream's steep
bank. But as he was swept along,
he suddenly saw before him what
looked like a big bundle of long
twigs to which he clung tightly.

Bella Donna raised her
broomstick and lifted her wet
white kitten out.

Aristotle was so out of breath that he could only manage a feeble mew. He clung as tightly to Bella Donna as he had to her broomstick, while she cuddled him close to make him feel safe again.

"Well, my boy," she said to him after she'd carried him home and rubbed him down, "you've managed to get through two lives in one go. The fall should have broken your little neck and the stream should have filled your little lungs. It looks as though it'll need a bit of magic to keep you in the land of the living. You really must take more care, Aristotle. Only five lives left now."

Chapter Four

Now time passed – quite a lot of time – without Aristotle getting into hot water, or cold water for that matter, or falling out of trees or down chimneys or into milk jugs, as he grew from kitten to cat.

Someone less wise than Bella Donna might have thought that he was over the worst of his troubles, but though Bella might have been old and skinny and ugly, she was also very wise indeed. She knew, in her wisdom, that her white cat would surely have other lives to lose, and so she kept a close eye on him.

Aristotle had grown used to the fact that Bella was mostly around the place by day and that usually she went out at night, leaving him snoozing by the kitchen fire. Being a sharp-eyed animal, he also noticed that she never went out into the darkness without her broomstick, though he did not know why.

By day, Bella Donna was a busy person, so that, try as she would, there were times when the eye she kept on Aristotle was not as close as it should have been.

For example, she often seemed to be heating something – Aristotle did not know what – in a large black cauldron that hung suspended over the kitchen fire. Whatever was in this cauldron needed a lot of stirring, and one day, while Bella was busy at this, Aristotle slipped out for a walk.

For some time he had been
curious – as all cats are – about a lot
of loud noises that came, now and
again, from one side of the wood.
There were clanking noises and
puffing noises and sometimes a
shrill whistle, and they got louder
and louder as whatever-it-was drew
nearer, and then quieter and quieter
as whatever-it-was went away.

On this particular day, what
with the crackling of the fire
and the bubbling of the liquid in
the cauldron, Bella did not hear
the clanking and the puffing, but
the whistle, when it came, was
very loud and very shrill. She
looked quickly round the kitchen
for Aristotle but there was no sign
of him.

Had anyone been watching, they
would have been amazed at how
swiftly Bella now acted. First she
dropped her ladle into the cauldron.

Then she lifted the cauldron off the fire. Then she picked up her broomstick from the corner and dashed out.

It had taken Aristotle a good five minutes to get from the cottage and up the embankment to the railway line, but Bella positively flew there in no time at all – to see a terrifying sight.

On the railway track a white cat was walking, sniffing curiously at the steel lines on either side of him, unaware that behind him an old steam train was coming into view, puffing and clanking and now, at sight of the cat, whistling like mad.

Like a lot of white cats, Aristotle was a bit deaf, and he didn't take notice of the noise until

the engine was nearly upon him,

but then he heard Bella's voice.

"Lie down, Aristotle!" she screeched. "Lie down flat and don't move a whisker!"

Never did Aristotle forget the terrible noise as the puffing whistling engine and its clanking rattling coaches passed right over him, only inches above, it seemed, as he lay between the rails.

(Never, what's more, did he ever go on the railway track again.)

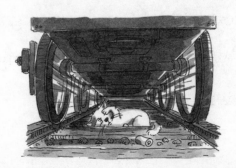

As the noise died away, he opened his eyes which, in his terror, he had kept tight shut, to see Bella Donna leaning on her broomstick by the edge of the track, and he ran to her and began to rub himself against her legs.

"Well, my boy," she said to him, "that was a near thing, wasn't it? Good job you stayed still like I told you. You want to watch out, Aristotle. Only four lives to go now." And she gave him a long look with her beady eyes.

Chapter Five

At the lower end of Bella Donna's
wood there was a farm, to which
Bella went to buy milk and eggs.
Behind the farmhouse was a yard,
and in the middle of the yard there
stood a big wooden dog kennel.
Now that Aristotle was nearly
full grown, he often walked
down to the farm behind Bella,
his white tail waving.

The first time he went there, she stopped at the yard gate and pointed to the kennel.

"Don't go near that," she said to him, "or you'll be sorry. You wait here while I go and see the farmer's wife."

On the next few visits, Aristotle did indeed sit by the gate, staring at the dark opening in the kennel until, one day, he thought he'd like to have a look inside it, and he set off across the yard.

As he got near, he smelt a
strange smell coming from it,
a smell that he'd never come across
before and didn't much like, and
then, when he was very close, he
heard a noise. It was the noise of
someone snoring.

Curious, as all cats are, Aristotle
poked his head round the edge of
the kennel door and peered into
the blackness of the interior.
There, fast asleep,
lying on its
stomach,

its great head upon its paws, lay
a very large animal – the cause of
the smell and the snores.

It so happened that Aristotle
had never before in his life seen
a dog, and did not know that most
dogs don't much like cats. But the
smell of this animal was now so
strong in his nose and its snoring
so loud in his ears that he thought
he'd leave it in peace, especially
as each snore drew back the
creature's lips to show a battery
of sharp-looking teeth.

Just as well, for this was not only a large dog but a very fierce dog, which the farmer kept to guard his farmyard. Round its thick neck was a heavy studded leather collar and, attached to this collar at one end and to a ring-bolt in the kennel at the other, was a length of stout chain.

Little did Aristotle dream that this chain would soon save him from losing the last four of his lives in one fell swoop.

For the next couple of visits

to the farm with Bella, Aristotle contented himself with just sitting and staring at the smell-filled snore-loud kennel. But then, one day, he decided that, while Bella was buying her eggs and milk, he must just have another peep at the strange animal.

As before, he peered into the darkness within. As before, he saw the great sleeping shape. But then something very unfortunate happened. Maybe it was the dust from the dog's straw bedding,

maybe it was to do
with the smell of the creature,
but suddenly Aristotle sneezed.

Afterwards he could never
clearly remember what happened
next, but Bella Donna, coming
out of the farmhouse carrying a
jug of milk and a basket of eggs,
dropped the lot at the sight
which met her eyes.

With a volley of bloodcurdling growls, the big dog came hurtling out of its kennel, inches behind a wildly-fleeing white cat which it overtook and grabbed in its huge jaws.

But the dog's rush took it to the end of its length of chain. Suddenly brought up short, its head was jerked back, forcing its jaws open, and out of them fell a bewildered

befuddled bedraggled Aristotle.

Back in the cottage, once Bella Donna had cleaned him up and satisfied herself that there were no bones broken, she addressed him in stern fashion.

"Well, my boy," she said, "you should have listened to me, shouldn't you? That was a close shave. You want to watch your step, Aristotle. Only three lives to go."

She held him up before her face and looked into his pale eyes. Gazing back into her dark twinkling ones, Aristotle forgot his fright and snuggled thankfully against his friend.

Chapter Six

Aristotle never went into the farmyard now. He would walk part of the way with Bella when she went to buy milk and eggs, but at the edge of the wood he'd stop and wait until she came back again.

Sometimes he would hear the barking of that awful monster that lived in the kennel but he had no wish ever to see it again.

Then one day, months later,
he did.

Bella was crossing the yard on
her way to the farmhouse when
she saw the farmer go to the kennel
and unclip the chain from the dog's
collar. It then lumbered towards
her, not in a threatening way but
with flattened ears, a wagging tail
and a sort of silly grin on its
great face.

"Funny thing,"
the farmer said
to her.

"Old Gripper, he's a devil with most people – bite 'em as soon as look at 'em, he will – but he seems to like you."

"I expect," said Bella, "that that's because he knows I'm not scared of him." And she put out a hand to the dog and he slobbered over it.

"I'm letting him have a little run round this morning,"

the farmer said. "There's some boys been scrumping apples out of my orchard. Old Gripper'll soon see them off."

For a while the dog sniffed about among the apple trees and then, making the most of the unaccustomed freedom, went towards the wood, his mind on rabbits.

But it was not a rabbit that saw him coming. It was a white cat.

At sight of the dog, Aristotle forgot all about waiting for Bella and took to his heels. Made silly by fright, he did not run back to the cottage but simply set off through the trees as fast as he could, without thinking where he was going. Seeing the railway embankment on one side and not wishing to go there again, he turned in the opposite direction, making, though he did not know it, straight for the road that ran along the other side of the wood.

Another thing he did not know was that he was being followed.

White is not the best colour for an animal that wants to conceal itself among the greens and browns of woodland, and it was a flash of white that caught Gripper's eye as he left the orchard. Breaking into a lumbering run, he came to the spot where he had sighted the cat. It was nowhere to be seen, but the dog put down his nose and began to follow the scent.

Someone else was following him.

Bella Donna was coming back through the farmyard with her purchases when she saw the dog at about the spot on the wood's edge where she had left her cat. Quickly she shoved the milk jug and the egg basket under a bush and grasped her broomstick.

Aristotle meanwhile had reached the twisty road that ran beside the wood. Thinking that he had outpaced the awful

monster and so feeling less scared,

he stopped to get his breath.

But then he looked up the road

to see another monster coming –

a large lorry.

As he turned to get away from

the nasty noisy thing, he came face

to face with Gripper, who had

been running silently on his
trail and now dashed at him,
open-mouthed.

"Never seen anything like it
in my life before," the lorry

driver told his wife later. "There's this white cat, runs clean under my lorry, between the wheels and out the other side, and then there's this big dog, been chasing the cat, and he tries to follow, and I bangs on my brakes, and then suddenly there's this old woman, appears from nowhere, she does, and she's carrying what looks like a broomstick, and she gives the dog a great whack with it, and he lets out a howl and runs back into the wood, and I gets out and there's no sign of any of 'em, cat, dog, old woman, all disappeared."

"She had a broomstick, you say?" asked the lorry driver's wife.

"Yes."

"Go on with you! Next thing, you'll be telling me she was all dressed in black, with a tall black hat on her head!"

"She was."

Once he had got over his

double fright of being chased

by one monster and almost

squashed by another, Aristotle

managed somehow to make his

way home to the cottage, to find

Bella Donna at the kitchen fire,

stirring something in the cauldron.

On the table stood a jug of milk

and a basket of eggs. In the corner

stood her broomstick.

He ran to her and began to

rub himself madly against her

black-stockinged legs, purring

like a steam engine.

"Well, my boy," said Bella Donna, "that was a narrow squeak. I think we have to count that as two lives. Dog or lorry – either would have killed you, Aristotle. So really, out of your nine lives, you've used up eight now. Your ninth life is going to have to last you a long, long time."

She picked up her white cat and stroked him thoughtfully.

"And I'll tell you something, Aristotle," she said to him, "I shouldn't be at all surprised now if it did."

Chapter Seven

When Bella Donna next went
down to the farm, leaving Aristotle
behind of course, she went straight
to the dog kennel in the yard.

Gripper came out with a rush,
only to pull himself to a halt
before the chain did, once he
saw who it was. Bella tickled
him behind his ears and he
wagged his tail madly.

"I've come to say I'm sorry,"
Bella told him. "I shouldn't have
whacked you with my broomstick.
Mind you, if I hadn't, you'd have
run under the lorry. But I must
have hurt your feelings as well
as your bottom. Will you forgive
me?" For answer, the big dog
grinned at her and licked her hand.

Now not just
the months but the
years passed, and
Aristotle grew
into a fine cat

and a sensible cat what's more. He didn't get into any scrapes and, as Bella had foreseen, he kept healthy and stayed safe, happy in his long ninth life.

Dogs, however, have only one life, and down at the farm Gripper had grown very old. No longer did he rush out of his kennel at the approach of strangers. No longer did he try to bite anyone and everyone. Mostly he lay in the yard at the end of his chain, thinking of days gone by.

One warm night he lay there, still, in the light of a full moon, and had the strangest of dreams.

In this dream he heard a swishing noise in the sky above and, raising his heavy head, looked up to see a dark shape flying across the face of the moon. It seemed to be riding on something, this dark shape did, and to have on its head a tall black hat. Sitting perched on its shoulder was a white shape, a shape that reminded Old Gripper of something that had happened years ago. He gave one last great growl before his head dropped upon his paws, never to be raised again.

Strangely, when Bella next went down to the farm, Aristotle followed her as of old, white tail waving. He followed her right into the yard and right past the dark mouth of the kennel. Stretched out from its door, the long chain lay on the ground and at the end of it was the heavy studded dog-collar, unbuckled.

Chapter Eight

I expect you're wondering if
Aristotle is still enjoying his ninth
life? Well he is, I can tell you,
because he's now not only a
grown-up cat but he's a proper
witch's cat too, helping the good
witch Bella Donna with her work.
Some of the strange mixtures that
Bella heats in her cauldron each
day are food for her and for her cat.

But many are magic potions for curing ailments, such as headaches or toothaches or tummyaches.

At night Bella climbs on her broomstick and flies off – Aristotle knows this because he goes with her – carrying these medicines to the homes of sick children, where she gives a spoonful of this or that to the child as it sleeps. Afterwards she always makes sure that she and her cat are home by midnight.

Aristotle's quite an old fellow now, of course, and Bella Donna is an old old woman. Her grey hair is as white as the fur of her cat.

But they're still living happily together in the old thatched cottage in the wood. Bella Donna and Aristotle have still got a lot of time to enjoy one another's company.

Dick King-Smith (1922–2011), a former dairy farmer, is one of the world's favourite children's book authors. Winner of the Guardian Children's Fiction Prize for *The Sheep-pig* (filmed as *Babe*), he was named Children's Book Author of the Year in 1991 and won the 1995 Children's Book Award for *Harriet's Hare*. His titles for Walker include *The Twin Giants*, *Lady Lollipop* and its sequel, *Clever Lollipop*, *My Animal Friends*, *The Twin Giants* and the much-loved *Sophie* series.

Bob Graham has written and illustrated many acclaimed children's picture books, including *How to Heal a Broken Wing*; *Max*, which won the 2000 Smarties Gold Medal; *Jethro Byrde, Fairy Child*, which won the Kate Greenaway Medal in 2002; *April Underhill, Tooth Fairy*, which was shortlisted for the Kate Greenaway in 2011; and *A Bus Called Heaven*, which is endorsed by Amnesty International UK and was the winner of the 2012 Children's Book Council of Australia Picture Book of the Year Award – a prize Bob has won an unprecedented six times. He lives in Melbourne, Australia.